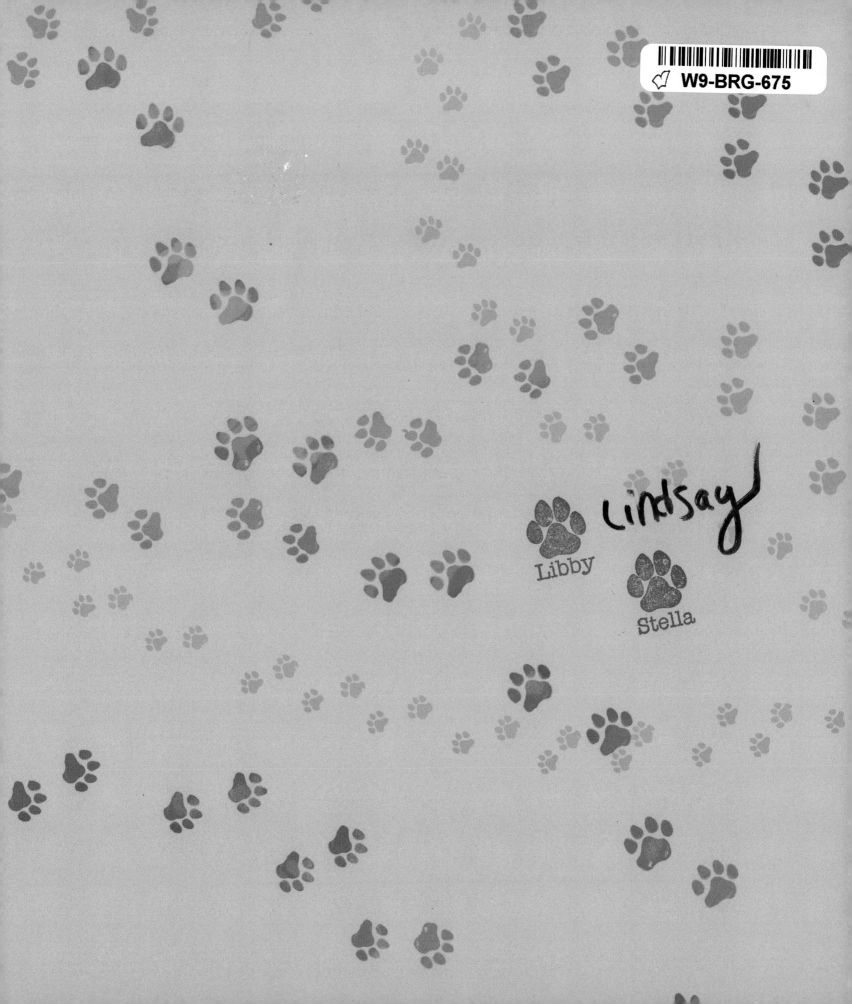

Libby

Lindsay

Stella

Libby's Adventures To the Creek

Written by Lindsay Golz
Illustrated by Megan Hagel

Illustrated and designed by Megan Hagel

ISBN 13: 978-1-59298-727-6

Library of Congress Catalog Number: 2016906936

Printed in the United States of America

First Printing: 2016

20 19 18 17 16   5 4 3 2 1

Beaver's Pond Press, Inc.

7108 Ohms Lane

Edina, MN 55439–2129

(952) 829-8818

www.BeaversPondPress.com

To order, visit www.ItascaBooks.com or call (800) 901-3480. Reseller discounts available.

This book is inspired
by Lindsay's best friend, Libby.

Once upon a time, there was a golden retriever named Libby, who loved going on adventures.

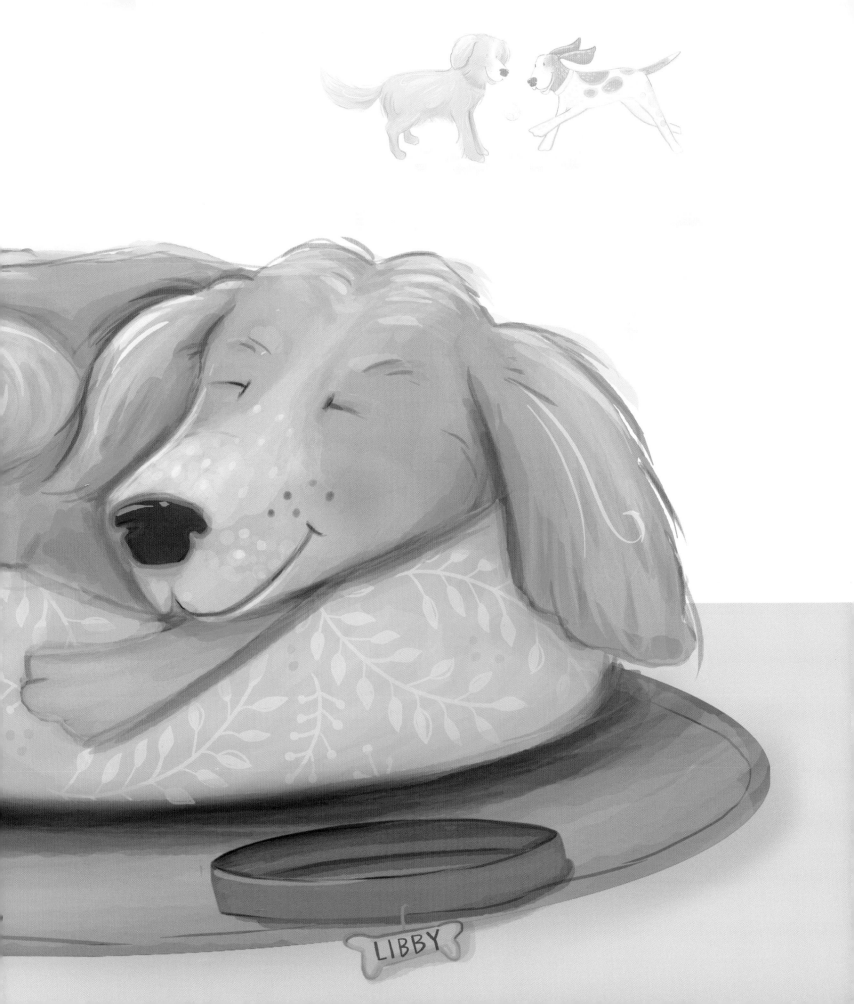

One early summer morning,
Libby woke up and stretched
out her body, taking in the bright
sunshine before running outside
to greet all her neighbor friends.

LIBBY

Libby woofed and woofed until she heard each of her friends woof a greeting back. Then Libby woofed once more, asking her friends what adventure they should **embark** on that day. They all agreed: it was perfect weather for a day at the creek.

Libby was so excited: Minnehaha Creek was her favorite place! She quickly ran back into the house to get her special swimming collar. Then she jumped over the fence and onto the sidewalk, where her friends would soon join her.

Yaggy came running out of the white
house with her tiny tail wagging so fast.
Sisters Blizzard and Sage bounded out of
the big, brown house, in step with each other.

As the dogs got closer to the creek, their wild friend Stella joined the crew. The five friends were so happy to be together, they gave each other high fives all around.

They stopped on their way to say hi to Roxie Raccoon. Libby stuck her nose into Roxie's house and she jumped out to say "Good morning!"

Sammy Squirrel heard Libby and the gang and slid down his tree. Sammy was gathering nuts with his buddies, but they took a break to say hello to the dog pals.

The friends sniffed each other and Libby said to the squirrels, "We're heading down to the creek. Why don't you come along?" The excited squirrels agreed.

At the creek, Stella jumped in first, making a huge splash!

The others jumped in and joined her.

Then they each jumped
onto a lily pad
and paddled to the
tennis courts.

Libby and Stella found tennis balls in the weeds and Sage ran them up to the courts.

While the dogs played tennis,
the squirrel party sat in
the trees and cheered.

Blizzard was the grand champion and pranced around the court with a bone Roxie had given them to be the grand prize.

The dogs were panting after their tennis match, so they jumped back into the creek to cool off. As they floated under another bridge, they stopped to say hello to Danny and Dixie Duck. The ducks quacked, "Hey, dogs, let's play tag."

The dogs chased the ducks up and down the creek.

The ducks laughed and quacked loudly because nobody could catch them, not even speedy Yaggy.

After the game, the dogs jumped back onto their
lily pads and Libby led the gang down the creek.
They went under a log and around
a sandbar to their favorite hill.

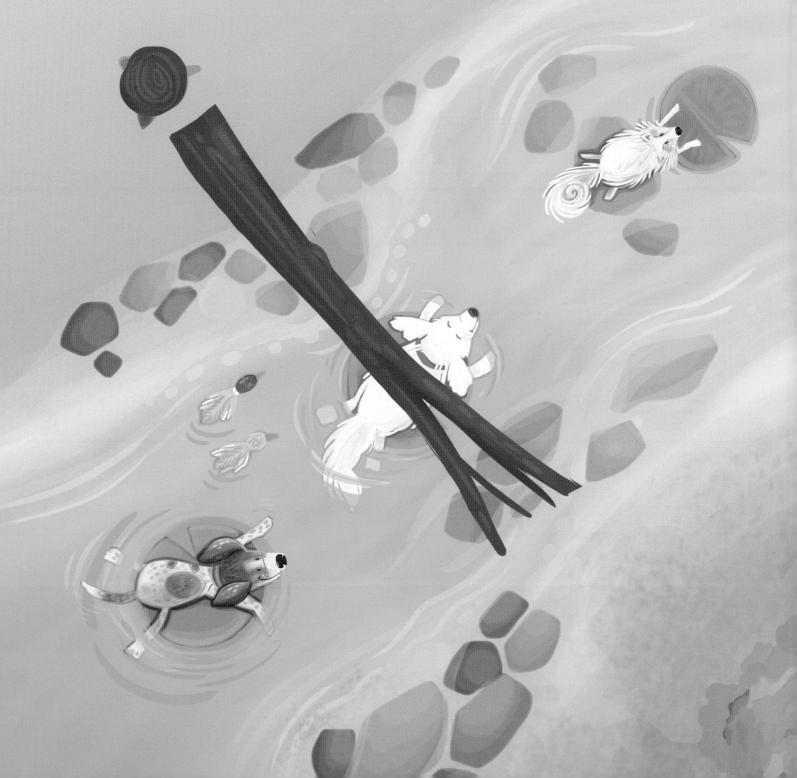

Then spunky Libby jumped out of the creek and ran up the hill as fast as she could, finding that Roxie Raccoon and Sammy Squirrel had surprised them with a picnic.

Libby barked to Stella, "Come fast! There's a magnificent picnic for us!" The dogs ran and the ducks flew with them to join the feast.

The animals shared their favorite treats while laughing and chatting about their fun day.

It was starting to get dark—time for the animals to go back!

Libby gave everyone a big hug and thanked them for going on the great adventure to Minnehaha Creek with her.

When Libby got home, she lapped up some water and then jumped into her bed. She smiled as she thought to herself, every adventure is always better with special friends.

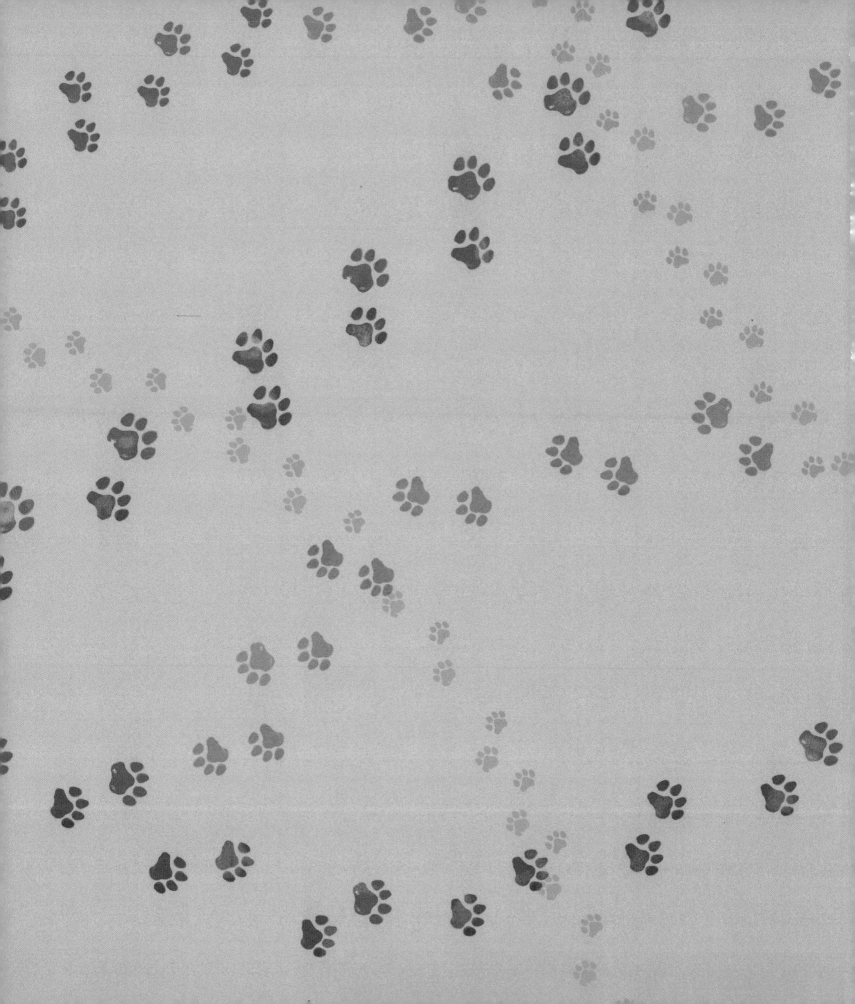